ALF ™

THE GREAT ALFONSO

Written by Roxanne Ruth-Stephens
Illustrated by Eldon Doty
Cover by Ken Kimmelman

CHECKERBOARD PRESS ◆ NEW YORK

TM & © 1987 Alien Productions. All rights reserved. "ALF" and "ALF" characters are trademarks of Alien Productions. Licensed by Lorimar Telepictures Distribution, Inc. Printed in U.S.A. Published by Checkerboard Press, a division of Macmillan, Inc. CHECKERBOARD PRESS and colophon are trademarks of Macmillan, Inc. ISBN 0-02-688554-9

Brian and ALF were watching TV together. Brian had just seen something very exciting.

"Wow, Dad!" Brian called to Willie. "Look — the circus is in town! Can we go? Please, please, please!"

"Oh, Brian," said Kate, his mother.
"You guessed our surprise. We're all
going to the circus this afternoon."

ALF jumped up. "Yeah! I think I'd like
the circus, too!" He pointed to the TV set.
"All those extra-large pussycats!"

Kate took ALF into the kitchen to talk to him.

"Now, ALF. You know you can't go to the circus with us. Everyone would wonder who — or what — you are!"

Kate could see that the little alien's feelings were hurt. She gave him a hug.

"I have an idea!" she said. "You can make your favorite everything-on-it pizza while we're gone. Just promise not to mess up the kitchen — I mean, the whole house."

ALF watched the Tanners leave. He was annoyed. "This is unfair to aliens," he said to himself. "Earthlings have all the fun! Hmmm. I don't need them to take me. I'll check out this 'circus' thing by myself. I can be back before Kate and Willie come home."

ALF borrowed one of Brian's jackets and slipped out the back door.

ALF followed a crowd of people to the circus entrance. The popcorn and cotton candy smelled wonderful! Suddenly a guard stopped him.

"Hey, little fellow! That's some costume! I think you want the other entrance."

ALF saw a tall clown with orange hair and long green shoes opening the door.

"No problem!" ALF said to the guard. "That must be where all the best-looking people go in!"

ALF found himself backstage. Never had he heard such noises or seen such excitement. All around him were people with funny painted faces and glittery clothes.

A baby elephant wiggled his trunk at ALF. ALF wiggled his nose at the elephant.

"Hey!" said ALF happily. "You remind me of my cousin!"

The ringmaster, however, was not happy about anything. He was groaning and moaning.

"The head clown is sick," he cried. "The show can't go on without him! What will we do? We're ruined!"

And just then the ringmaster spotted ALF.

"Oh, thank goodness!" laughed the ringmaster. "The substitute clown has finally arrived! Get him into his costume, and be quick about it!"

Then he hurried away through the animals and cheering performers.

"We're so glad you made it in time," said a clown to ALF. "Sorry you didn't have time to get out of your other costume first."

The circus parade marched into the arena. The ponies pranced. The clowns tumbled. The wild animals roared. The ringmaster waved proudly to the audience. Everyone cheered! ALF could sense the excitement. This was much more fun than making a pizza!

ALF could see children laughing and pointing at him. Everyone was clapping and waving. He realized that he was a star!

"Wow!" thought ALF. "I could get used to this!"

"Kate!" shouted Willie, as he pointed to the chariot.
"Isn't that amazing? There's a clown who looks a little —
no, a lot — like ALF!"

Brian stared hard at the little clown. Then he smiled and
smiled. Brian knew.

ALF's chariot stopped in the center ring. The ringmaster bent over and spoke to ALF. "Quick, fella! What's your name?"

ALF thought for a moment, then he mumbled to the ringmaster.

The ringmaster stood up tall and spoke into the microphone. "And now, ladies and gentlemen, girls and boys! Introducing . . . THE GREAT ALFONSO!"

And while the drums rolled, the ringmaster led ALF — the Great Alfonso — over to a big springboard. He pointed. "Sit here."

ALF had seen children playing on seesaws. It looked like fun. So he sat.

All of a sudden, ALF was up in the air!

"Whoa! What's happening?"

Everything had happened so quickly!

"Hey!" said ALF. "Next time, give me a little warning! I need time to practice being a bird!"

The pretty trapeze artist gave ALF a big hug. "You were wonderful!" she said. "And now . . . jump!"

She took ALF's hand and they soared again, this time down to the safety net. They bounced like rubber balls.

The crowd clapped and cheered. "Hooray for the Great Alfonso!" they shouted.

The ringmaster shook ALF's hand and said, "Bravo! You were magnificent! The Flying Faloneys always start their act with that routine. They believe it's good luck. They wouldn't have gone on tonight without the head clown on the springboard. You saved the show, Alfonso!"

The Tanners arrived home from the circus. The first thing they saw was ALF on the sofa.

"ALF!" said Willie. "You look so tired. What have you been up to?"

The next thing they saw was the pizza.
"Ooh, look!" cried Lynn. "ALF,
did you make that all by yourself?"

"ALF! It looks so clean! Why, there's not even a crumb! How did you manage to make a pizza without making a mess?"

"Yo! Let's eat," said ALF. "You'll never know what I
went through to get that pizza done in time."